Build-Your-Own
TOOLBOX 1-2-3!

Wood Glue

Property of
FAMILY OF FAITH
LIBRARY

by Kimberly Weinberger • Illustrated by Edward Miller

Cartwheel
B·O·O·K·S·®

SCHOLASTIC INC.

New York   Toronto   London   Auckland   Sydney   Mexico City   New Delhi   Hong Kong

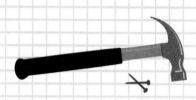

Text written by Kimberly Weinberger.
Illustrations by Edward Miller.

ISBN 0-439-28859-2

10 9 8 7 6 5 4 3 2 1   01 02 03 04 05

Printed in the U.S.A.   24
First printing, November 2001

With all the fixing and building they do, tools are probably the most useful items found in a home. That's why they deserve a special box all their own—a toolbox!

Toolbox

Bottom (C)

End (D)

Side (A)

Side (B)

End (E)

Dowel (F)

Building a wooden toolbox is a great project for you and a grown-up to do together. The first step is to gather all of the materials you'll need. You can buy all of the necessary components at The Home Depot®. Or, if you prefer, you can buy a complete Home Depot toolbox kit with pre-cut, pre-drilled wood and all of the necessary nails and screws at Toys R Us®. If a kit is not available, a grown-up will need to measure and cut the following pieces of wood:

One piece of pressed board

$10\,^3/_8$" x $4\,^1/_4$" x $1/_8$"
(26 cm x 10.8 cm x 0.3 cm)

Pressed board is made from shredded wood pieces that are pressed together.

One wooden dowel stick

$10\,^3/_8$" long x $1/_2$" in diameter
(26 cm x 1.3 cm)

A dowel stick is a rounded stick of wood with flat ends.

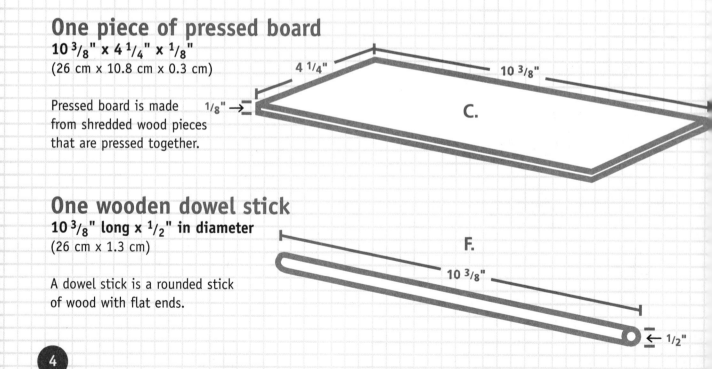

Two pieces of wood
10" x 3" x ¹/₂"
(25 cm x 7.6 cm x 1.3 cm)

Cut a long slot along the face of the wood. The slot should be ¹/₈" (0.3 cm) wide and ¹/₈" (0.3 cm) deep. It should begin ³/₈" (0.9 cm) from the bottom edge of the wood.

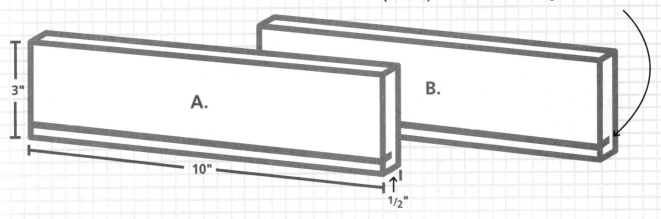

3"

A.

B.

10"

¹/₂"

Two five-sided pieces of wood
bottom 5" wide (12.7 cm)
sides 3 ¹/₂" (9 cm)
upper sides 4 ¹/₄" (10.8 cm)
³/₄" thick (1.9 cm)

Drill a shallow hole into the top of the piece. The hole will not go all the way through the wood. It should begin ⁵/₈" (1.6 cm) from the pointed top of the piece. It should be ¹/₂" (1.3 cm) in diameter and ¹/₄" (0.6 cm) deep.

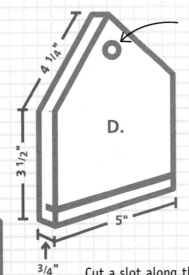

4 ¹/₄"

3 ¹/₂"

D.

5"

The upper sides should come to a point, like a triangle. Round out the top edge with sandpaper.

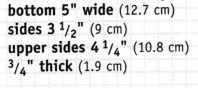

E.

³/₄"

Cut a slot along the bottom of the piece on the same side as the hole. The slot should be ¹/₈" (0.3 cm) wide and ¹/₈" (0.3 cm) deep. It should begin ³/₈" (0.9 cm) from the bottom edge of the wood.

Once you have all of your wood pieces, it's time to collect the rest of your materials and tools. You will need:

Wood Glue

This product usually comes in a plastic squeeze bottle. The glue is specially made to stick to wood surfaces.

Nail Claw Hammer

Your hammer should have a steel head and a strong handle to grip. One side of the hammer's head should be a V-shaped claw. This side will remove any nails that might bend during hammering.

Eight 1" (2.5 cm) nails

You might want to have a few extra nails on hand as well. Nails can sometimes bend if they're not hammered correctly.

Sandpaper

This is a sheet of paper with fine, medium, or coarse grains of sand covering one side. For this project, a medium-grade sandpaper should be used. (You may want to include a sanding block to hold the sandpaper. Sanding blocks provide good leverage and a level contact surface.)

Goggles

When working with tools, you should always wear goggles to protect your eyes.

Safety Rules

You now have all of the materials and tools needed to start building your toolbox. ***But wait!*** Before you begin, it's important to review the safety rules that are part of any building project.

1.

Wear goggles.

Goggles protect your eyes from flying dust and other dangerous particles.

2.

Always work with an adult.

Tools and materials like hammers and nails can be dangerous if used the wrong way. Never use a tool without a grown-up to watch over you.

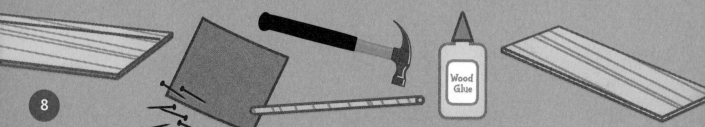

Wood Glue

3. Work on a hard, solid surface.

To hammer wood correctly, you'll need to place your wood pieces on a strong surface for support. Find a sturdy worktable or a hard floor to work on this project.

4. Work slowly and safely.

Pounding the tiny head of a nail can be tricky at first. Rushing may cause your hammer to slip and pound your thumb instead of the nail—*ouch!* Be extra careful and take your time. Your fingers will thank you!

By following all of these safety rules, you'll be an expert in no time. So turn the page and let's start building!

Step 1

- Hold your pressed wood piece in front of you. This will be the bottom of your toolbox.

- Slide the edge of this bottom piece into the slot of one of the 10" x 3" (25 cm x 7.6 cm) pieces of wood. This will be one side of the toolbox. The bottom piece is longer. It should stick out from the end by $1/4$" (0.6 cm) on each side.

- Slide the other edge of the bottom piece into the slot of the second 10" x 3" (25 cm x 7.6 cm) piece of wood. This is the opposite side of the toolbox.

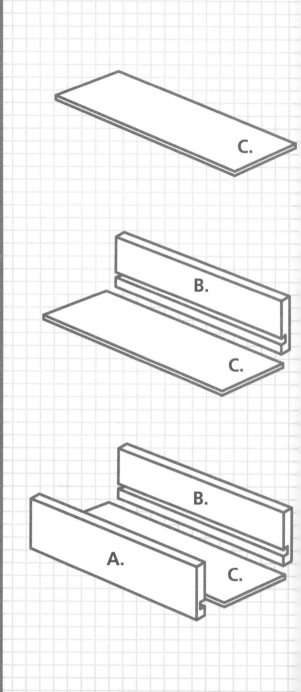

By joining these three pieces, you've now formed Section One. Place this section off to the side. Don't worry if the pieces slide apart a bit. They'll be joined together with nails later.

Step 2

- Place one of the five-sided wood pieces in front of you. The side with the hole and the slot should be faceup. This piece will be one end of the toolbox.

- Squeeze a drop of glue into the hole of the wood piece. Be sure *NOT* to squeeze too hard! Only a small amount of glue is needed.

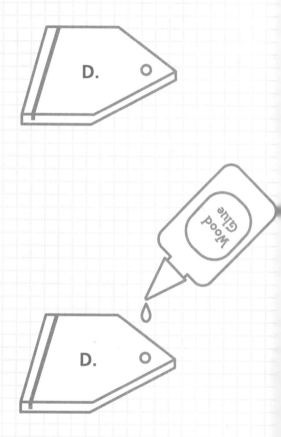

- Pick up the 10 $^3/_8$" (26 cm) dowel stick. Place one end into the glued hole of the wood piece. With the piece on a table or other hard surface, press the dowel stick firmly into the hole.

- Place the second five-sided wood piece in front of you. This will be the other end of the toolbox. Gently squeeze a drop of glue into the hole of this piece.

- Place the hole on the dowel stick and press firmly.

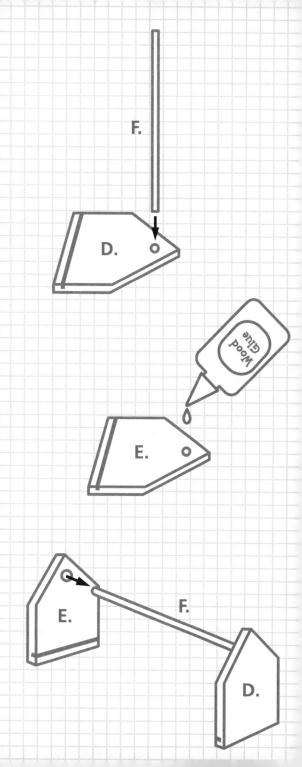

The dowel stick and the two end pieces have now formed Section Two.

15

Step 4

- Place Section One in front of you. This is the section that was formed by the bottom and side pieces.

- Pick up Section Two. Gently spread the bottoms of the two end pieces apart. The dowel stick should remain firmly in the holes.

- Slowly lower Section Two onto Section One. The bottom of the toolbox should fit into the slots of the two end pieces. Gently press the ends and sides of the toolbox together. The bottom piece should fit into the slots of the two side pieces and the two end pieces.

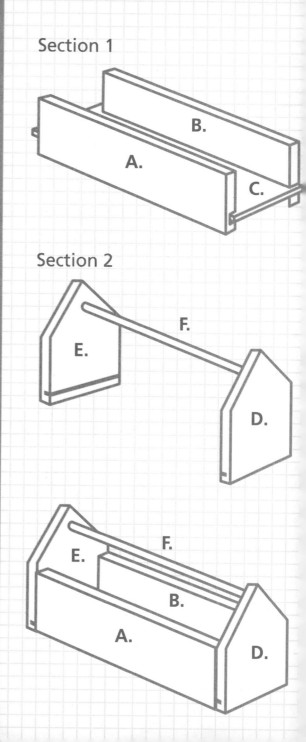

Section 1

Section 2

Step 5

- Stand your toolbox on one end. Place it on a hard surface. Be sure the sides, ends, and bottom are lined up correctly.

- Hold a nail in one hand. Place the tip of the nail near the lower corner of the toolbox's end. Be sure that the nail is in a good position. It should connect the end to the side piece when it is hammered in completely. Try not to position the nail too close to the edge.

- With your hammer in your other hand, firmly strike the head of the nail until it stands securely on its own.

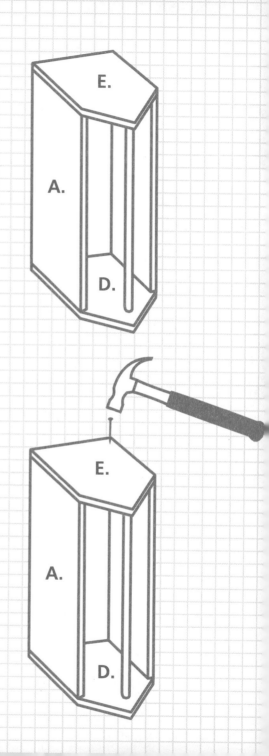

- Using the same technique, hammer a second nail into the opposite bottom corner of the same end.

- When the second nail is in place, gently press the sides, ends, and bottom piece together again. Hammer a third nail into the upper corner of this same end.

- Finish this end of your toolbox by hammering a fourth nail into the opposite upper corner.

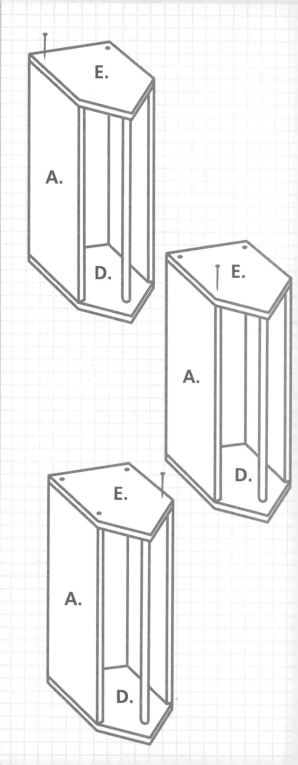

After hammering each nail, check to make sure that the sides, ends, and bottom piece of your toolbox are still lined up correctly. The pounding of the hammer may have caused the pieces to shift.

Step 7

- Turn your toolbox over so that the nailed end is on the bottom. Check that the pieces of the top end are lined up correctly.

- As with the first end, place a nail on the lower corner of this end of your toolbox. Is the nail positioned well? Be sure that it is not too close to the edge.

- Strike the head of this nail with your hammer.

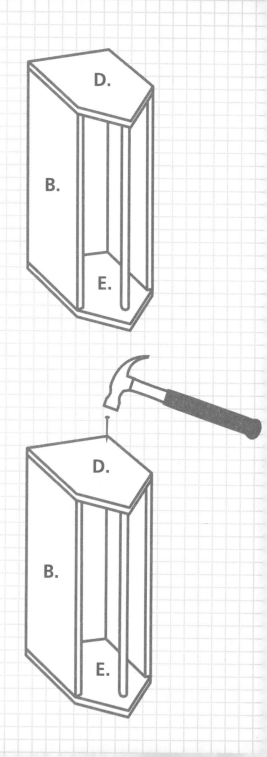

If the nail is not going in straight, use the V-shaped claw side of your hammer to remove it. Hammering takes lots of practice. *Don't give up!*

- By now, your toolbox should be much less wobbly. Line up any pieces that may have shifted during hammering. Hammer a second nail into the opposite lower corner of this end.

- Finally, hammer your final two nails into the two upper corners of this end.

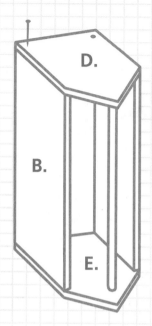

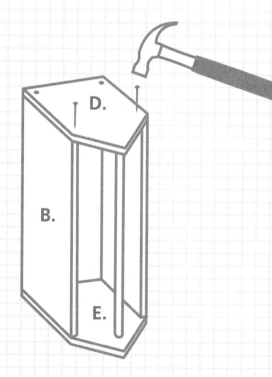

Congratulations!

You've built a toolbox! Now you're
ready for the finishing touches.

Step 9

• The wood you have been using is probably rough around the edges. To make your toolbox smooth, gently rub your sandpaper along any splintered spots.

> Sandpaper works best when you rub at a steady pace—not too fast, not too slow. Try rubbing in small circles as you go. Before you know it, your toolbox will be smooth and splinter-free!

This last step is optional. If you like the natural wood of your toolbox as it is, then you've finished your project. Great work!

If you'd like to decorate your toolbox, there are many ways to dress it up.

Ask a grown-up to help you paint your box any color you like. Be sure the paint is completely dry before putting any of your tools inside.

Stickers and markers can also add some fun, final touches to your toolbox. Spell out your name, or glue on pictures. It's all up to you!

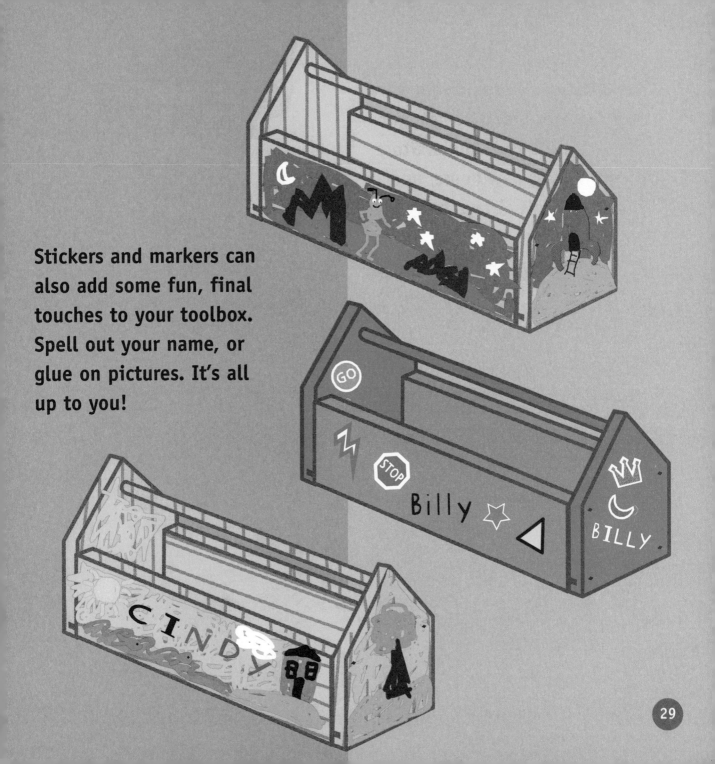

Now that you've built your very own toolbox, you'll always know where to find your tools. Store them in their new home, and your tools will always be ready for any project.

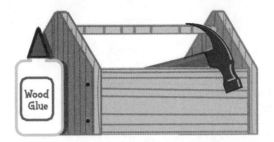

THE HOME DEPOT®
PROJECT AWARD

_____

(Fill in your name)

successfully built a wooden toolbox on

_____

(Fill in date)